This edition published by Parragon Books Ltd in 2014 and distributed by

Parragon Inc.
440 Park Avenue South, 13th Floor
New York, NY 10016
www.parragon.com

Copyright © Parragon Books Ltd 2013–2014

ISBN 978-1-4723-5203-3

Printed in China

The
Wind
in the
Willows

Based on the original story by Kenneth Grahame

Retold by Catherine Allison

Illustrated by Victoria Assanelli

Bath · New York · Singapore · Hong Kong · Cologne · Delhi
Melbourne · Amsterdam · Johannesburg · Shenzhen

The Mole had been working very hard all the morning spring cleaning his little home. Spring was moving in the air, filling even his dark and lowly little house with longing. It was small wonder, then, that suddenly he could bear it no longer. He scraped and scratched and scrabbled and scrooged, working busily with his little paws till at last, pop! His snout came out into the sunlight.

He rambled happily across the meadow until he came to the river. Never in his life had he seen a river before—a sleek, sinuous, full-bodied animal, chasing and chuckling. The Mole was bewitched.

In the bank opposite, he noticed a dark hole. As he watched, one eye then another appeared, on a small, brown face with whiskers, neat ears, and thick, silky hair. It was the Water Rat.

"Would you like to come over?" asked the Rat.

He stepped into a little boat and rowed smartly across before helping the Mole to step gingerly on board.

"Believe me," said the Rat, "there is nothing half so much worth doing as simply messing about in boats."

They rowed gently on for a while, but soon Mole was so excited by the light, the sound, and the smell of the river that he cried out, "Ratty! Please, I want to row, now!"

And though the Rat tried to stop him, the Mole jumped up to seize the oars, the boat tipped, and—sploosh! Both animals were in the water.

Poor Mole! Rat helped him to the bank while he coughed and spluttered, feeling thoroughly ashamed of himself. But when Mole started to apologize, Rat laughed. "What's a little wet to a water rat? Why don't you come and stay with me for a little time? I can teach you to row and to swim, and you'll soon be as handy on the water as any of us!"

So Mole went to stay in Rat's comfortable waterside home.

"Ratty," said the Mole suddenly, one bright morning, "if you please, won't you take me to call on Mr. Toad? I've heard so much about him, and I do so want to make his acquaintance."

"Why, certainly," said the good-natured Rat. "Get the boat out, and we'll paddle up there at once. It's never the wrong time to call on Toad. Always good-tempered, always glad to see you, always sorry when you go, he is!"

"He must be a very nice animal," observed the Mole, as he got into the boat and started to row.

"He is indeed the best of animals," replied the Rat. "He does have his crazes, though. Once, it was nothing but sailing. He bought sailing boats, sailing clothes, sailing everything! Then he tired of that and took to houseboating, and we all had to stay with him on his houseboat and pretend we liked it. He was going to spend the rest of his life on a houseboat. It's always the same, whatever he takes up. He gets tired of it and starts on something fresh."

Rounding a bend in the river, they came in sight of Toad Hall, a handsome old house with lawns reaching down to the water's edge. They disembarked, strolled up to the house, and found Toad resting in a lawn chair.

"Hooray!" Toad cried upon seeing them. "I was just about to send a boat to fetch you. I've discovered what I want to do for the rest of my life."

Rat sighed and looked knowingly at Mole.

Toad led them to the stable yard, where he pointed to a gypsy caravan painted a canary yellow with green and red wheels. A horse was already harnessed to it. "That's the only way to travel!" cried Toad. "The open road, the dusty highway, the rolling hills! Here today, up and off to somewhere else tomorrow! All complete inside with everything we'll need when we make our start this afternoon."

Rat needed to be persuaded to leave his beloved river for another of Toad's crazes, but later that afternoon, the three friends set off.

It was a golden afternoon. The friends spent several hours rambling happily along narrow lanes in Toad's caravan.

It was not till much later that they came out on the high road. They were now strolling along easily, chatting together happily, when far behind them they heard a faint hum, like the drone of a distant bee. A faint "Toot-toot!" wailed like an uneasy animal in pain. Glancing back, Toad and Rat saw a cloud of dust with a dark center of energy. It was advancing on them at incredible speed, but not knowing what it was, they simply continued their conversation.

In an instant, the peaceful scene was changed. With a blast of wind and a whirl of sound, "Toot-toot!" rang in their ears, and a magnificent motorcar, immense and breathtaking, with its driver tense and hugging the wheel, roared down upon them, flung a cloud of dust around them, then dwindled to a speck in the far distance.

The horse, who had been dreaming of his quiet paddock, suddenly reared, plunged, and though Mole tried to stop him, drove the caravan backward into the deep ditch by the side of the road. It wavered an instant; there was a heart-wrenching crash—and the canary-colored caravan, their pride and joy, lay on its side, a total wreck.

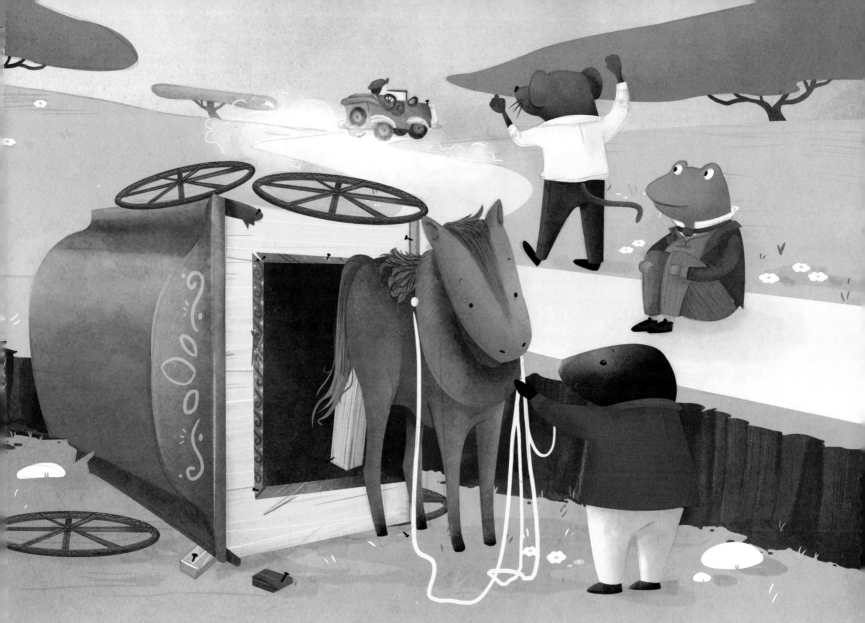

Rat hopped up and down, shaking his fists, while the Mole tried to quiet the horse. Toad, however, sat in the middle of the dusty road and stared after the disappearing motorcar, faintly murmuring, "Toot-toot!"

"Now that's the only way to travel!" he sighed. "Freedom to go wherever you want, as fast as you want!"

"What are we to do with him?" asked Mole.

"Nothing at all," replied the Rat. "He has got a new craze and will be quite useless for all practical purposes."

They carried Toad to the nearest town, arranged for the caravan and horse to be picked up, and took the first train home.

After their adventure with Toad, life for the Mole and the Rat settled back into its peaceful ways again. But then Mole asked to meet another of Rat's friends, Mr. Badger, who lived in the middle of the deep, dark Wild Wood.

"Badger's a shy animal and doesn't leave the Wild Wood often. He'll turn up some day or other, and I'll introduce you," said the Rat. But the Badger never turned up, and late one December afternoon, while the Rat dozed, the Mole decided to go and find him.

When he first stepped into the Wild Wood, twigs crackled under his feet and logs tripped him, but that was all fun and exciting. But then the faces began to appear: little, evil, wedge-shaped faces, looking at him. Then the whistling began: very faint and shrill, far behind him, then far ahead of him. And then the pattering began: the patter of little feet. The whole wood seemed to be hunting now, closing in around the Mole. He began to run, until eventually, exhausted and terrified, he took refuge in a hollow.

When Rat woke up, he realized that Mole was not at home. Fresh tracks outside led directly to the Wild Wood, and Rat was worried. The Wild Wood animals could be dangerous. He put on his coat and set off to find his friend.

After an hour's searching, Rat found
Mole, huddled in the hollow. The light had
nearly gone, and Rat was anxious to start for
home, but Mole was too weak and scared to move.
By the time Rat had comforted him and urged him to
begin the journey back, there was thick snow on the
ground. The wood looked completely different. The
friends struggled on for an hour or two, but they
became hopelessly lost. Then the Mole tripped on
something under the snow and stumbled.

"What was that?" said the Rat, looking at the
ground. He dug in the snow and uncovered a metal
scraper for cleaning boots. After further digging in the
snow bank, Rat found a door with a bell pull and a
brass plate engraved with the words "Mr. Badger."

Rat and Mole rapped on the door until it opened to reveal a long snout and a pair of small, blinking eyes.

"Ratty, my dear man!" exclaimed the Badger on seeing his friend. "Come in, both of you! Out in the snow and in the Wild Wood, too!"

The two animals tumbled over each other in their eagerness to get inside, where Badger offered them a large, warm kitchen, a roaring fire, dressing gowns, slippers, and safety.

When they had eaten dinner, Rat and Mole told Badger about their evening's adventures. Badger nodded gravely. Then he asked them about Toad.

"The rumor on the river is that he's going from bad to worse," said the Rat. "He's had seven cars and seven smashes, been in the hospital three times, and as for the speeding fines he's had to pay ...."

Badger thought hard. "I can't do anything in the winter," he said, "but in the spring, we—that is, you and me and our friend the Mole here—we'll take Toad seriously in hand. We'll make him a sensible Toad, by force, if need be."

Rat and Mole slept soundly that night. Mole felt so at home in Badger's comfortable burrow—it reminded him of his own underground home—and he told Badger so.

"Once underground," Mole said, "nothing can happen to you, and nothing can get at you. Things go on overhead, and when you want to, up you go, and there they are, waiting for you."

The Badger simply beamed at him. "That's exactly what I say," he replied. "By the way," he said confidentially, "I'll pass the word around the Wild Wood, and you'll have no further trouble from the inhabitants. They're not so bad, really. And anyway, any friend of mine walks where he likes!"

By this time, Rat was eager to get back to his river. So goodbyes were said, and Badger took the friends through underground tunnels to the very edge of the wood. Then they set off for home, firelight, familiar things, and the beloved river.

Mole and Rat did not see Badger again until early the next summer, but when he turned up, he had Toad on his mind.

"I have heard," he said sternly, "that Toad is to have a new and exceptionally powerful motorcar delivered today. You must come with me instantly and save him from himself."

When the friends got to Toad Hall, a shiny new motorcar stood outside, and Toad, dressed in goggles, cap, and enormous gloves, was looking very pleased with himself. When Badger suggested that he should give up motorcars for good, Toad refused with great spirit. Badger then turned to the chauffeur in charge of the car and said, "I'm afraid that Mr. Toad has changed his mind. He does not want to buy the car."

The chauffeur drove it away, and Rat and Mole hustled the protesting Toad into his bedroom and locked the door. There he stayed, under lock and key, guarded day and night, for several weeks. It was the only way to stop Toad from buying another car and getting into trouble.

As time passed, Toad's car madness appeared to be under control. But in fact, he was planning his escape. One day, when his captors were otherwise occupied, he dressed himself in a smart suit, filled his pockets with cash, and escaped out of his bedroom window, feeling pleased with himself.

Toad was about halfway through lunch at a local inn when he heard a car turn into the yard. He had not seen or driven a car for weeks, and he couldn't stop himself. The next moment, he had stolen it and was sitting in the driver's seat, revving the engine and speeding through the open country! He sped he knew not where, not caring what might happen to him.

When he was caught, Toad was arrested and charged with stealing and with driving dangerously. He was also rude to the police, which didn't help his case. The judge sentenced him to twenty years in prison.

Toad flung himself on the floor of his cell in despair. "This is the end of everything," he said. "At least, it is the end of Toad, which is the same thing." Day after day, he cried and howled, and refused to eat or drink.

Then one day, the jailer's daughter, who was very fond of animals, knocked on the door of his cell. "Cheer up, Toad," she said. "I've brought you some tea and toast." Toad sat up and saw the toast, dripping with golden butter. He took a bite and a sip of tea while the girl asked him about himself. Soon, he felt much better.

Over the following weeks, the girl began to feel sorry for Toad. One morning, she said, "Toad, I have an aunt who does the washing for all the prisoners here. She takes it out on Monday and brings it in again on Friday. Today is Thursday. I believe I could disguise you in her dress and bonnet tomorrow, and you could escape. You're very alike in many respects—particularly about the figure."

"We're not," said the Toad in a huff. "I have a very elegant figure."

"So has my aunt!" replied the girl.

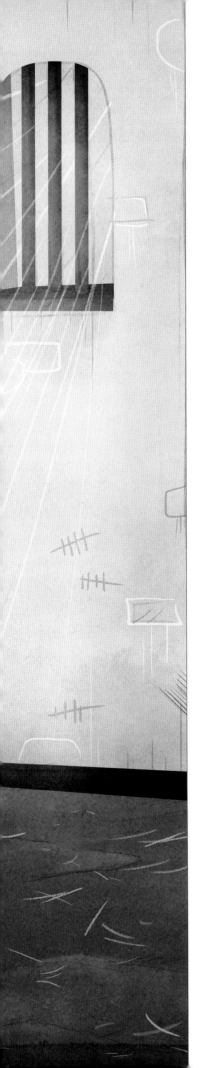

Though Toad thought it beneath him to dress as a washerwoman, this was a great opportunity, so he agreed to the plan.

The next evening, the girl ushered her aunt into Toad's cell. The girl helped Toad put on a cotton gown, an apron, a shawl, and a black bonnet.

"Goodbye, Toad," she said, "and good luck!"

With a quaking heart, Toad set forth on what he thought would be a most hazardous adventure. But to his surprise, everything was remarkably easy. The washerwoman's outfit seemed to be a passport for every barred door and gate. At last, he heard the great outer door click behind him and knew that he was free!

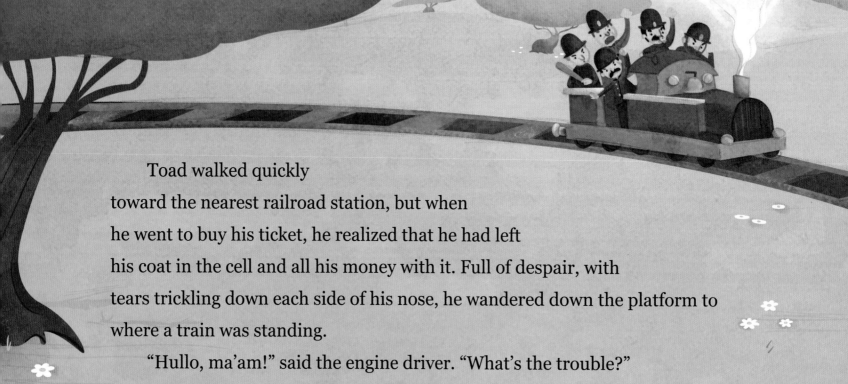

Toad walked quickly toward the nearest railroad station, but when he went to buy his ticket, he realized that he had left his coat in the cell and all his money with it. Full of despair, with tears trickling down each side of his nose, he wandered down the platform to where a train was standing.

"Hullo, ma'am!" said the engine driver. "What's the trouble?"

"Oh, sir!" said Toad. "I've lost all my money and can't pay for a ticket, and I must get home tonight somehow."

"Well, I'll tell you what I'll do," said the driver. "If you'll wash a few shirts for me when you get home and send 'em along, I'll give you a ride on my engine."

Toad scrambled up into the cab. The train moved out of the station and its speed increased, every moment taking Toad nearer to Toad Hall. But after some time, another engine appeared on the rails behind them, crowded with policemen waving and shouting, "Stop, stop, stop!"

"Save me, dear kind Mr. Engine Driver!" pleaded Toad. "I am not the simple washerwoman I seem to be! I am a toad—the well-known and popular Mr. Toad— just escaped from a loathsome prison." When the engine driver listened to Toad's crimes, he said, "You have indeed been a wicked Toad. But the sight of an animal in tears makes me feel softhearted. So cheer up! We may beat them yet!"

They piled on more coal to speed up, but still their pursuers gained on them.

"There's one thing left," said the driver, "and it's your only chance. There's a long tunnel ahead and thick woods on the other side. When we are through, I will put on the brakes, and you must jump out and hide. Then I will go full speed again, and they can chase me if they like."

When the driver gave the word, Toad
jumped, rolled down a hill, scrambled into the
woods, and hid. Out of the tunnel burst the
other train, but Toad fled farther into
the woods, leaving the railroad as
far behind as possible.

Toad found a safe spot in the woods and fell asleep. He awoke the following morning in bright sunlight. He marched forth, cold but confident, hungry but hopeful, along a rustic road, which was soon joined by a canal. A long, low barge boat soon came along the water. On the deck stood a strong-looking woman.

"A nice morning, ma'am!" she remarked to Toad.

"I daresay it is, ma'am," said Toad politely, "but I've lost all my money and my way! I need to get to Toad Hall."

"Why, I'm going that way myself," replied the bargewoman. "I'll give you a ride."

"You're in the washing business, aren't you, ma'am?" said the woman thoughtfully, as Toad stepped lightly on board. "There's a heap of my clothes in the corner of the cabin. If you'll just take one or two and wash them as we go along, why, it'll be a real help to me."

Toad was worried. He fetched the washtub and soap, selected a few pieces of clothing, and started to wash. A long half hour passed, and every minute of it saw Toad getting crosser and crosser. Nothing he could do to the clothes seemed to get them clean.

The bargewoman started to laugh at him. "You've never washed so much as a shirt in your life!"

"I would have you know that I am a very well-known, distinguished Toad, and I will not be laughed at by anyone!" said Toad in fury.

"Why, so you are!" cried the woman, moving nearer. "A horrid, nasty, crawly Toad! And in my nice clean barge, too!"

She caught him by one front leg and one hind leg, and suddenly, Toad found himself flying through the air.

He landed in cold, deep water that swept him swiftly along into a river. There was a big, dark hole in the bank above his head, so he caught hold of the edge and held on. Something was inching toward him in the hole. A face gradually became clear and familiar. Brown and small, with whiskers ... it was Rat!

Rat gripped Toad firmly and pulled him inside his home. Then he sent Toad upstairs to wash and put on fresh clothes. "Never in my whole life have I seen a shabbier, more disreputable object than you, Toad!" he cried.

When he had changed, Toad started to tell all his adventures, dwelling mainly on his own cleverness. But the more he talked and boasted, the more silent Rat became.

"I don't want to give you pain, Toady," said Rat, "but do you mean that you've heard nothing about the ferrets and stoats and weasels, and how they've taken over Toad Hall?"

"No! Not a word!" cried Toad, trembling in every limb.

"When you got into trouble, the Wild Wood animals said that you would never come back. One night, they moved into Toad Hall and declared they were there for good. They've got guards all around, and they're all armed. Mole and Badger have been watching them and planning how to get your house back."

There was a knock at the door. It was Mr. Badger, closely followed by the Mole. They were both shabby and unwashed but greeted Toad warmly. Then they described the situation up at Toad Hall.

"The ferrets and stoats and weasels make the best guards in the world," said Badger solemnly. "But I've got a great secret. There's an underground passage that leads from the riverbank into the middle of Toad Hall. There's going to be a big party at the Hall tomorrow night—it's the Chief Weasel's birthday, I believe—and all the weasels will be gathered in the dining room, eating and drinking with no weapons at hand. The guards will be posted as usual, but the passage leads right up next to the dining room, so we don't need to worry about them."

"So we shall creep in quietly," cried the Mole.

"With our swords and sticks!" shouted the Rat.

"And rush in upon them!" said the Badger.

"And give them the fright of their lives!" cried the Toad.

Toad went off to bed, thinking that he was too excited to sleep. But he found the sheets and blankets very friendly and comforting after having slept on plain straw on a stone floor in a drafty cell, and he soon began to snore happily.

He awoke late the next morning to find that the other animals had finished breakfast some time ago. Rat was running around the room busily, with his arms full of equipment of every kind. He was distributing them in four little heaps on the floor, saying excitedly under his breath, "Here's-a-stick-for-the-Rat, here's-a-stick-for-the-Mole, here's-a-stick-for-the-Toad, here's-a-stick-for-the-Badger! Here's-a-rope-for-the-Rat ..." and so on, while the four little heaps gradually grew and grew.

When it began to get dark, the Badger took a lantern in one paw, grasped his stick with the other, and led the others into the secret passage. They shuffled along until the Badger sensed that they were nearly under the dining room at Toad Hall. Such a tremendous noise of stamping feet and shouts of laughter was going on above that there was little danger of being heard. They hurried along till they were standing under a trapdoor.

"Now, boys, all together!" said the Badger, and the four of them put their shoulders to the trapdoor. "Get ready, all of you! The hour is come! Follow me!"

They flung the door wide open.

My! What a squealing and a squeaking and a screeching filled the air!

Up and down the hall strode the four comrades, whacking with their sticks and swiping with their swords and sending their surprised enemies scattering. In five minutes, the room was clear. Through the broken windows, the shrieks of fleeing weasels could be heard. The Badger, resting on his stick, wiped his brow. Mole made sure that the stoat and ferret guards had run away, too, then the four friends celebrated their victory in great joy and contentment with what remained of the Chief Weasel's feast.

The following morning, all the animals agreed to have a banquet to celebrate their victory in the Battle of Toad Hall. Toad's job was to write the invitations. "You must do it," said Badger. "You own Toad Hall, after all, so you're the host."

Toad didn't want to write boring letters when he could be swaggering around the Hall enjoying himself! But then he had an idea. He would write them and mention his leading part in the fight, and how he defeated the Chief Weasel, and he would hint at his adventures and triumphs!

Badger was suspicious about Toad's change of heart, so when the invitations were ready for posting, Rat opened and read a couple.

"They're disgraceful!" he told Badger. "Full of pride and swagger. Toad doesn't realize that he has done anything wrong in his life!" So Mole rewrote the invitations, and Badger and Rat solemnly took Toad aside and told him how bad he had been.

At last, the banquet arrived. All the guests cheered Toad and congratulated him on his courage, his cleverness, and his fighting qualities. But Toad only smiled faintly and murmured, "Not at all! Badger was the mastermind; the Mole and Water Rat bore the brunt of the fighting; I did very little."

The animals were puzzled by his modesty, and much to Toad's surprise, he realized that he didn't need to brag to be the center of attention. Badger and Rat stared at him open-mouthed, giving him the greatest satisfaction of all.

In fact, Toad became such a reformed character that the police dropped the charges against him. Though life became peaceful again, the brave actions of the four friends were not forgotten. Sometimes they would stroll through the Wild Wood, now successfully tamed. As they passed, mother weasels would say to their young ones, "Look, baby! There goes the great Mr. Toad, the gallant Water Rat, the famous Mr. Mole, and next to him, the fearsome Mr. Badger!"

Of course, the friends were not fearsome warriors at all, but it made them chuckle to think that they might be considered so.